I0733460

THE CONIUM REVIEW
vol. 10

James R. Gapinski
Managing Editor

Elle Nash
Contest Judge

Cassie Birk
Fiction Editor

Uma Rallabhandi
Fiction Editor

[contents]

THE CONIUM REVIEW

vol. 10

Conium Press
Portland, OR

The Conium Review
Vol. 10
© 2021 Conium Press
Portland, OR

http://www.coniumreview.com

ISBN-13 978-1-942387-18-3
ISSN 2164-6252

Cover Image: © plherrera / licensed through iStock
Layout & Design: James R. Gapinski

[contents]

SQUALOR

Erica Kent

SQUALOR

Erica Kent

I truck in squalor. It's how I roll. It's not going too far to say squalor. A pretentious boy I brought home once called my place macabre, or as he said "Boschian." He found the mess ironic because of my neat appearance (plated hair, Peter Pan collar, accordion skirt) so I chased him away. Real squalor's not ironic. Real squalor's something to be valued. Inside my shack is where it lives:

A trove of crumbs. Serious crumbs. Crumbs that crust up and clump together. A colony of crumbs. Old crumbs, young crumbs. Toasts crumbs, cereal crumbs. Look at all the crumbs. I nibble at them, testing their grit. They taste like history.

Also, grime. Linoleum grime. Underside grime. Behind the toilet grime. Grime on grime.

Plus mold. Fuzzy, bluish mold. Kitchen sink mold. Shower ceiling mold: black stars on a gray sky. Mold that tastes like mold.

And clutter. Dusty and piled like a crazy genius' desk except there's no crazy genius only a silly person with garden variety mental illness who's managed to shove a bit into the mouth of the horse of despair just enough to ride a good, long while. Clop, clop, clop the hooves canter over vast, dirty terrain.

I truck in squalor. Squalor and scratching. But I'm not alone. Because mice. Behind the refrigerator. Mice in the walls. Mice in the basement. Well-fed, plump mice. If I could catch one, I'd take a bite of its tail. I bet it tastes like lye. Scritch-scratch-scritch, the mice say. They might be dumb, but they know a good thing when they see it. They know squalor like the backs of their little hands.

THE DRAWDOWN

Lyndsie Manusos

THE DRAWDOWN

Lyndsie Manusos

It wasn't long before a hole opened up just in front of Stratton Lock on the Fox River and began to gulp down the rest of the Chain o' Lakes. The Fox Waterway agency said it made no goddamn sense; a single hole could not swallow a whole expanse of lakes in northwest Illinois, but there it was, and down it chugged.

The hole took a speedboat or two before the line of boaters waiting to go down river past the dam realized what had happened. They revved their engines, their motors coughing smoke, and went back the way they came, heading upriver to the nearest piers in panic. The nearest lake bar, Mookies, was filled to the brim for the first time in years. (It was known they only served diluted tap beer, and the town hated them for it, and they hated the town in turn. But somehow, they managed to suck in regulars from year to year, so it was good business.)

My family's lake house held the nearest pier after Mookies. It was a small pier, holding a lift for our pontoon boat and two waverunners that my parents bought years ago off a distant relative that we never used. Boaters heading from the dam hurriedly tied to ours. My parents, trying to be good Samaritans, let them.

Within hours, the water level of the river dropped. Boats sagged and tugged on our pier posts. People huddled in our yard. My mother was wary of letting anyone use our bathroom, and my father hoped no one would sneak into the boat house and steal his stash of good gin. He didn't know I had watered down a few bottles myself, wanting to taste fire in my throat after long, hopeless nights.

Sneaking around was something I did rather well.

My first kiss was with a girl who lived on Grass Lake. Her family had a cigarette boat, painted a bright sunflower yellow, and after dinner at her house, we snuck out to their pier, climbed under the boat cover, and played Bullshit on the boat's fiberglass floor. She leaned over and kissed me when I called Bullshit on her claim of two aces, because I had the aces. All of them. She laughed and leaned in, and I was never so glad to have such fullness in my hands.

It's gone, it's all gone, someone yelled.

It's true, the water had receded further, gelatinous mud and trash taking the place of a tea-colored river. I shouldered past everyone and sat on the edge to witness. Bluegill swam against the current in their haste to escape. I heard sirens. I thought of other memories I'd had on the Chain o' Lakes: When I was a toddler, my father used to throw me from the back of the pontoon to my mother, who was in the water. I had always squealed as my mother caught me. The water smelled sweetly of grass and gasoline.

Later, when I was twelve, a boy was decapitated by a propeller while tubing downriver during Fourth of July weekend. It happened just beyond our pier, and my father was tempted to lock me in the house while police attempted to recover the body, the head. I remember peeking out my bedroom window, which faced the river, fearing and anticipating with a sort of thrill that I'd be the one to find it. To see bobbing eyes peer back at me and *see* and *see* and *see*—

I watched my feet dangle from the pier, the water sinking beneath my toes, and listed all the memories—pieces—I could think of, the kisses I had stolen, until it all became a current, a flow, a rush, like the bluegill swimming for their lives against the drain, the hole that would consume them, against the cacophony of screams at my back.

HUNTING FOR ELEPHANTS

Aimee Herman

HUNTING FOR ELEPHANTS

Aimee Herman

The movies reveal it like stew—red, thick, unmoving—but in real life, blood drips. It puddles and stains floorboards. That is why that rug is there. That is why the paper towels are always out. That is why Band-Aids flooded their body, becoming like another layer of skin. They were clumsy, rambunctious with their bodies, just doing what boys do.

Jurin and Joshua sat beside each other wearing one another's parts.

"We are beyond ourselves," Joshua, the older of the two, said.

It was Thursday, and the mourners were scattered around the living room. Slices of dried meat lay uncurled on mostly devoured platters. No one touched the coleslaw. The cookies were gone. When they got the call about their mother's death, the brothers had just finished wiping up their latest puzzle. They used to call it a surgery, but that felt too clinical, too impersonal. It lacked the romanticism of what it actually was: cutting into each other to mix and match their parts.

"We came from the same woman, the same body," Joshua had said a few years in. "The cells I lived on, then fed you."

It started simple enough.

When Joshua was six and Jurin was four, Joshua took his teeth to his knuckle and bit down as hard as he could. He felt the rip of skin make way toward the iron bitterness of blood.

"Okay, now it's your turn," Joshua instructed his brother. "And then, you can give some of your blood to me and I to you."

It didn't get gruesome until several years later when Joshua was twelve and Jurin was ten. By then, they shared practically everything: clothes, favorites (movies, food, outdoor sports), and secret crushes. Their father had left early on, so it was just their mother. She was their secret crush. How can one live for nine months inside someone else and not have intense feelings for them? Their early fights gravitated toward her as they battled for her attention until one day Joshua came up with a plan.

"Let's just become one."

"I don't—I don't understand."

"If we combine all our parts, then when she is looking at you, talking to you, she is also looking at and talking to me," Joshua said. "We'll be—what's that word—when Mom cuts images from her magazines and then creates a picture from them? A collard?"

It was on this day, they walked to the kitchen and opened up the drawer of knives. Juris grabbed the bread knife because of its "shaky blade," and Joshua grabbed the electric knife usually reserved for Thanksgiving, Christmas, and Easter.

"Let's start on our left hands in case we run into any problems."

Juris was too nervous to start, so Joshua leaned in toward his brother and said so calmly, "Give me your favorite finger, so it can live on me. I'll give you my pointer."

Joshua mumbled, "Timberrrrrrrr."

When Juris's finger had completely detached, Joshua placed it gently on the floor as though it were alive, as though it were a child napping.

It wasn't until four years later that Juris could cut Joshua in that way, so Joshua took the bread knife and sawed and sawed and sawed away at his own finger.

"Stubborn bone."

Joshua wasted no time taking dental floss (cinnamon flavored) and sewed Juris's pinky onto his own hand replacing his pointer. He then used the rest of the floss to sew his favorite finger onto his brother in the space that now throbbed with blood.

During dinner that night, Joshua carefully explained to their mother that they shared an accident while trying to climb a tree in the backyard playing their favorite game, Hunting for Elephants.

Mother looked at both her sons and placed worry onto their shoulders. "Sometimes I wish I could put you both back inside me and protect you from everything trying to remove you from this world."

Both brothers looked at each other and smiled. They wished the same.

After the funeral, Joshua and Juris attempted small talk with various relatives and friends of their mother.

"There is a place," Aunt Fi said, "where bodies are buried in rented ground. After three years, the family has to dig up the bones of their beloved—with the hopes that decomposing has run its course. You know sometimes the flesh and strands of hair are still there—to make room for more bodies. But your mom, she can rest now. She was in so much pain toward the end."

Juris just looked at her, not quite knowing how to respond.

"What happened, dear?" Aunt Fi looked down at Juris's wrist (the latest puzzle). An almost perfect square of skin had been stretched out to replace the almost perfect square that Joshua had cut out and now wears on his wrist.

"I fell, minor patchwork, all good."

"Aunt Fi," Joshua interrupted. "Can I grab my brother for a minute?"

The brothers quietly walked upstairs toward their mother's bedroom, where many nights were spent beside her. The mourners gravitated toward the tables full of food, barely noticing their absence.

"I can't catch my breath," Joshua said. "I just—I want them all to leave so we can puzzle."

"Brother, I gotta take a break. I can still feel the throbbing in my wrist. Like some animal got caught beneath my skin and is heaving or something. Anyway, what is left? She's gone. We don't need to do this anymore."

Joshua looked at Juris as though he had started spouting a mystery language. "You think she is really gone? I still feel her. Here," he patted the bed. "And we can't stop until it's complete."

"Until what is complete?"

"*This*," Joshua flailed his arms around his body. "Until there is no part of us that doesn't belong to the other!"

When Joshua was nineteen and Juris was seventeen, they were puzzling several times a week. A vein plucked from one forearm and placed into the other; moles from Joshua scattered onto Juris; Juris's curls mixed with Joshua's thin strands, pieces of the other's scalp sewed in. Toes mixed and matched.

Joshua had been taking classes at community college while Juris finished his last year of high school. Juris wanted to attend a university out of state, to get a chance to experience life away from his brother and mother. He loved them to an unbearable degree, but he knew that the only way to live a true life, was to get away.

He told no one that he applied to a school on the opposite side of the country. When he was accepted, with the help of his guidance counselor, he filled out all the paperwork and made a plan to head west. He didn't tell his brother.

Hunting for Elephants started as Juris's idea. He and his brother loved to play games where all they needed was their imagination. They had plenty of toys, but what pleased them most was playing outside, making up various games that included secret handshakes and intricate plots.

They took turns being the elephant. The hunter took giant, deliberate steps around the backyard, carrying a heavy backpack filled with sandwiches (their mother always made them snacks to take on their "journey"), garden shears, and a makeshift rifle made of cardboard and tinfoil. Both brothers took this game very seriously.

But it didn't take long for Joshua to get bored. "Okay, I got you," he'd say, with pretend rifle pressed against Juris. "Now what?"

"I guess I can be hunter now?"

"Yeah, no, I have a better idea."

When they started to share blood, then skin, then body parts, they'd tell everyone around them that they were just playing Hunting for Elephants and that sometimes it got a little rough. Their mom never asked questions. They figured she was unaware. But she knew all along.

When Joshua was nine and Juris was seven, it was during Easter break and their mom was in the kitchen washing up after they feasted on honey ham, her famous extra creamy mashed potatoes, and trees from the forest (Juris's nickname for broccoli). The window right above the sink faced the backyard, and she loved feeling the warm water soften her skin while she watched her boys play so sweetly with each other. Then, she saw what Hunting for Elephants really entailed.

You want to know why she didn't stop them? Some behaviors are stitched into our bloodstream. Some behaviors will find us no matter how hard we try to run from them.

Joshua and Juris's mother was twelve and her sister was sixteen the first time it happened.

"I wanna give you a love letter," Fi said.

"Who's it from?"

"Me, silly. I love you. But if I give it to you on paper, I know you're gonna lose it. I want you to keep it forever."

"I will. I promise."

"Just hold still, okay? I'm gonna write it *on* you. Close your eyes and hold your breath. Hold it real long until you can't hold it any longer and then you can let it out. Got it?"

Joshua and Juris's mother idolized her sister and would have done anything she said. She craved Fi's love and attention, so she let as much air into her lungs as she possibly could. She closed her eyes. And then she felt the sharpest pain of her life.

Fi started to carve her love letter into her sister's left thigh with the box cutter that her parents used to open packages. "Every time you walk, my words will walk with you, okay? This is because I love you."

For the next two years, until Fi left for college, Joshua and Juris's mother allowed her sister to inscribe love letters into various parts of her body. After the blood, then scabbing, scars would form and create ghostly whispers of words, some legible but mostly unrecognizable. The sisters never told anyone.

When Joshua and Juris's mother met their father, she insisted on darkness each time they were intimate. Oftentimes, she tied him up, so he couldn't feel her skin. At first, he found this very arousing, but he soon grew tired of so many restrictions and left to make a new family. The boys never heard from him. Their mother decided her boys were enough love in this life, so she never searched for another man, another father for them. She became their everything.

Joshua and Juris's mother knew that she couldn't interrupt her boys' game because it was *their* love letter to each other. So, she looked away and never said a thing, giving them the privacy that she coveted with her sister.

"We should go downstairs. People are going to worry," Juris said.

"When you left, I almost couldn't recover. But I was with you, and you are always with me. All we've got is each other now."

"*That* was the last time," Juris said, with fingertips against swollen wrist. "And only because you begged, you threatened, you told me you'd kill—"

"When you left, I never stopped. I'd cut away parts of myself, wanting only *you* there. How does one just discontinue breathing and still be alive? Because that is what it felt like to me. Each cut, each puzzle, each time we became each other, I felt like I could actually catch my breath. And now she's gone and you—you're telling me you want to stop being my brother."

"I am not saying that. I am saying we are grown. I'm saying sometimes we do things when we think that is our only choice. I'm saying—"

"You're saying you never loved me! You are saying you never wanted any of this!" Joshua gestured at both their bodies, a pileup of scars.

"I'm saying Mom is gone now. We can be brothers without—without all of this."

"When you left for college, brother, I panicked. I just wish you had said something, I—"

"You wouldn't have let me go."

"I'd have gone with you. But I don't know, maybe

part of me understood. Except—I still yearned to play. To puzzle. To hunt—for elephants. And I—I did, brother. I did something bad. It was after class. I was walking along Burnside Avenue. I don't think she was a student. It all happened so quickly. I just—it was raining, or it was starting to rain. You know how the sky gets, like a villain in a movie. I wasn't thinking. I just lunged at her, sliced her—her cheek, maybe, I don't know, I kept walking. All this need in me to cut, to alter what exists, to rearrange. To make us one, for her, for us. I fell into a dark hole after that. I told no one, of course, but Mom could tell something had happened. She kept asking me, but I retreated. I pushed her out. That's when I left home. Left her. And then, the sickness. Maybe it was always in her, waiting until we stopped protecting her. It's my fault, brother."

Juris barely noticed that his brother had been holding a tiny razor blade in his palm. He had uncurled his fingers and it glistened like a silver icicle.

"I said no," Juris said, not allowing his eyes to dart away from the blade.

"It felt different to cut someone else. Someone I didn't know. It was meaningless like sex. Maybe it was just a scratch, maybe I barely made contact."

"I hear people leaving downstairs. We should say goodbye. We should—"

"And I just walked. For hours. Feeling the boxcutter inside my pocket, against my leg. Your leg."

"Some of them traveled a long distance, Joshua, we need to—"

"Strangely, I had this urge to keep doing it. Cutting every stranger that passed. Dulling the blade on their skin."

"Aunt Fi. She's going to wonder where we are. She's going to worry. I'm—"

"Just. Because. They. Weren't. You. All I wanted was you."

"Joshua, I'm leaving." Juris abruptly got up from the bed. His heart was beating its way out of his body.

"I never told you about Claudia." Joseph grasped onto Juris's wrist "She was in my math class in college, and we dated for exactly one month. Claudia puzzled too. She'd do it in class. I would watch her from the back of the room. No one else noticed or cared or whatever. Tiny droplets of blood on her palm, her forearm, I'd get so—" Joshua's voice trailed off. "Her face was so beautiful, it was covered in thick red and white scratches and scars. I'd never seen it so open before. You always wanted to hide our puzzles. Bandage them up. Claudia was—"

Juris jerked forward, freeing himself from his brother's grip. He opened the bedroom door and walked out.

"We are beyond ourselves," Joshua said, but no one else was left in the room to hear it.

BORN

Kaleena Madruga

BORN

Kaleena Madruga

1. I grew inside an egg on a white sand beach. Using my muzzle to break cracks in my home, I began to set myself free. I stretched and lumbered towards the ocean. The moonlight was my guide. I made it to the ocean and let my waves toss me to and fro until I found a current to ride. I floated effortlessly. The moonlight was my guide. The moonlight took me home.

2. I awoke to be the string of a red balloon tied to my mother's wrist. One day, the knot of my string became untied. I floated up into the heavens and glided away. Suddenly I felt myself becoming smaller, weaker. A few years later I fell towards the ground, only to land softly in the palm of my mother's hand.

3. I was in the cockpit of an international airplane. There were buttons, knobs, handles, and all other kinds of glowing, shining tools present to help me steer the plane. I am not a pilot. It was only me up there, I was alone in the sky. It was my job to choose a destination and get my feet safely planted back on the ground.

4. I became the hardwood floors of an ancient home covered in pet hair and dust. I would creak beneath your heavy steps. I would moan and groan, but no one would notice, thinking I was only the sounds the house sometimes makes at night. The paint-chipped walls, the old lace curtains, and the rusted beer cans on your table were me. I was the house that trapped me. I breathed through its walls.

5. I built a cottage in the woods. I planted sunflowers and a tomato garden. I tended to my babies, and I watched them grow. The sun released rays of glittering light on my cottage, and when it rained, I didn't mind. I got a book and a blanket; I read by the fire. Crackling embers and the smell of burning wood lulled me to sleep. My flowers grew and tapped their big full leaves against my window. They sang to me in the light of the day and said: *"we are okay, we are doing fine."*

THE SKY SAW US

Ted Hayden

THE SKY SAW US

Ted Hayden

When I woke up in your bed, Cassie, you were already dressed for work, hair wet from the shower, brown eyes regarding me skeptically.

"It's eight fifteen. Time to go."

Your feet were bare, your toenail polish red and chipped. You grabbed my t-shirt off the floor, threw it onto my chest, and waved at the window. "Looks like it might actually be kind of chilly today."

The top half of El Cozon's skyscrapers were gone, shrouded in clouds. This late in the summer, dawn fog should have been a distant memory. For weeks, morning had been just as bright as noon.

One of my sneakers was halfway under the bed, the other was on a pile of your unwashed clothes. I collected both, tightened their laces, and yelled goodbye through a closed bathroom door.

"Say *hello* to my ex-coworkers and *fuck you* to my ex-boss!"

"Hah!" A mouthful of toothpaste garbled your laugh.

As I walked outside, misty air dampened sound. Birds nesting in apartment gutters sang slowly. At a stoplight between a grocery store parking lot and a do-it-yourself car wash, a man with matted hair and torn jeans put down his cardboard sign. Ignoring the cars on the road, he looked up, confused. Clouds glinted like they were sewn with silver thread.

The light turned green. In rush-hour traffic, drivers accelerated cautiously, paying as much attention to the gray sky as to the cars ahead. An irrational nervousness kept me focused on the sidewalk. I studied how tree roots cracked through cement.

At the next stoplight, a thirty-something with a laptop case hanging off his shoulder turned to me.

"Look up, man. The sky's a—it's a fucking mirror."

Stretching from the roof of the house next to me to the hill of houses in the distance, the clouds had parted to show the city's reflection.

It arched and bent and twisted, like thousands of pharmacy security mirrors had been fused together. When I looked directly above my head, I didn't see myself looking down. I saw an old woman in another neighborhood sitting on her apartment patio. The sky showed hundreds of scenes. In one corner, children in a school playground jumped, trying to touch their upside-down doubles. In the next curve, a man frantically leaped into his car and accelerated onto the street. Even though the mirror was high above, it magnified reflections so I could see every detail.

My cell buzzed. It was a text from you, Arturo. "Work cancelled. Me and Cassie at Reds."

More people came out to the sidewalks as I walked to the bar. Some pushed through the crowds, panicked. Others moved slowly, mesmerized by the reflections.

You sat together at a corner table in Red's, cold Pilsners in your hands, a third glass waiting for me. The place was packed, and you shared your table with strangers. I pushed a squat stool next to you, Cassie, and rested my arm around the back of your chair.

The only sound in the bar came from televisions. A reporter interviewed a father as his wife and children lugged suitcases out of their house. "We're getting out of here. I don't want this thing falling on my kids."

The channel's traffic helicopter flew to the coast where fog rolled in. As it gained altitude, the cameraman leaned out of the door, pointing his lens up. Studio anchors asked questions. "Do you see anything?" "Careful. Go slow." "What's out there?" Billowing gray filled the screen. The pilot said he was turning around and heading inland. As he flew toward El Cozon, fog thickened.

An anchor reported that residents of foothill communities said that the mirror disappeared into a bank of clouds running along the mountains. On the other side of the range, the sky hadn't changed. It remained its normal, bright summer blue. Onscreen, a satellite photo showed a huge cloud over the city.

A man sitting at the bar raised his glass. Grabbing the shoulder of the woman beside him, he made a toast. "At least it's not so goddamned hot that my balls are sticking to my leg. Here's to silver linings!"

The stranger next to me ordered beers and shots for our entire table. "Hell, it hasn't killed us yet. Cheers to that," he said.

We knocked our glasses together and downed our drinks.

Arturo, you wanted to smoke. I followed you outside. Leaning against the bar's wall, you stared up at the reflection of a girl, maybe six years old, who wore pink jellies and stood in the mud. Her wide eyes looked at everything the sky showed her, moving from one point to the next, then freezing on us. She picked a twig off the ground, put it between her lips, and inhaled. When you took the cigarette out of your mouth, she did the same, copying your gesture, tapping her stick as you ashed onto the sidewalk.

The other smokers laughed. "Hey, we're being bad role models," said a man with a friar tuck bald spot and a thick mustache. "Can't smoke in front of a little kid. Put out your cigarettes!" It was a joke, but everyone smiled and stomped out their butts, waving at the girl in the sky. With a wide grin and a missing front tooth, she waved back.

You came out to join us, Cassie. We left the bar and went downtown, where the mirror was even more striking. Although it hung high over skyscrapers, we could see the logos on people's hats, the rings on their fingers, the colors of their eyes.

"Maybe it curves so that the images are magnified. Like, if we were right next to it, people's reflections would be as big as whales," I guessed.

"Maybe." Both of you shrugged. The more time we spent under it, the less any hypothesis seemed like it could explain what we saw. With offices closed and school cancelled, everyone who didn't leave the city stayed outside in cool summer temperatures, wandering from block to block, stopping to talk to people they had never met before, all of us feeling the same mix of wonder and fear. We watched the city watch itself.

The three of us walked for miles. That night, we stood on the beach, looking out over the ocean, where the fog never cleared.

. . .

I want to describe El Cozon to the people who will never see it.

As I write, our streets still stretch from the beach to the mountains. A dry river runs between skyscrapers. Years ago, before that river was cemented over, wandering priests stopped at its banks to set up a mission. They wondered why a place with rich soil and a temperate climate was so sparsely populated, not realizing that the strange terraced hills they climbed had been built by an indigenous metropolis, its population wiped out by smallpox and cholera only a few decades before the missionaries' arrival.

That dead city was what brought me to this living one. I came here fourteen months before the mirror did, to start a job in a museum's windowless basement sorting artifacts and helping curators prepare exhibitions. There, me and Cassie joked with you, Arturo, about how you refused to stop wearing the faded t-shirts and worn jeans that fit your college classrooms but made our bosses roll their eyes. Me and Arturo laughed at you, Cassie, because your thirty-five-year old boyfriend seemed geriatric to us, an old man who looked even older when he wrapped his arm around your waist. Both of you made fun of me for my clumsiness, crossing your fingers when I picked up an ancient clay bowl, mocking me when I came back from lunch with mustard on my shirt.

Between those conversations, we tried to work out what to write on the object labels that would be displayed next to the artifacts. The old city hadn't developed an alphabet. Its people spoke a language no living man or woman had understood for generations. Its memories were mute, hidden in lodges' buried foundations and shards of broken pottery. How could we describe a place that told us so little about itself?

. . .

The morning after the mirror appeared, the three of us were exhausted in my and Arturo's apartment, crowded around a laptop that had been streaming local news all night. At a morning press conference, a military meteorologist interpreted data drones had collected. Although she couldn't explain the phenomenon, she said its effects didn't diverge dramatically from those of an average cloudy day. The mirror absorbed some sunlight, cooled temperatures, and kept moisture in the air. There was no reason to panic. El Cozon's officials would monitor the situation. If anything changed, they would send an alert.

Before the clock hit noon, you both got texts from the museum. All curatorial staff still in the city had to come to an emergency meeting. I told you to hit me up after they let you out.

Cassie, when you met me in the park that afternoon, I was drinking a twenty-four-ounce Coors hidden in a paper bag. Three kids played on the bench next to us, indifferent to the meteorological mystery above their heads. The shortest of the bunch, a fuzzy-headed boy in a nacho cheese stained t-shirt, stood with one foot on the bench's seat and the other on its backrest. His skinned knee pointed at the sky. Ripping open a neon blue popsicle, he licked it.

"Look at me!"

He stuck his blue-stained tongue out at his friends

laying in the grass. They laughed and he turned his head to the sky, whooping in triumph. They shouted, "Wow!" and pointed at a curve in the mirror. "You can see us right there!" "Your tongue's in the mirror."

Cassie, you laughed as much as they did. Tearing open their popsicles, they turned their tongues blue, then yellow, then purple, mugging at their reflections, mocking the mirror that hung over our heads.

"It's weird," I said, "I remember doing that kind of stuff with my friends, going to our favorite parks, jumping off swings, but none of the little details. What did we say? What made us laugh? I have no idea."

You leaned against me, resting your arm on my leg. "Early onset Alzheimer's. Such a tragedy." Your hair was a mess of curls.

"Hey. Come on. I'm serious."

Looking up at me, you smiled. "Yeah, I know. When I was a kid, we used to play in the woods, all these different games. Some of them, we would make up insane, elaborate rules. I wish I could tell you what they were. But I don't have a clue."

"Exactly. I can still feel the emotion of it, though. Like a weight. Summers of hanging out and goofing off."

"You know what my favorite game was? A classic." You stole my beer and slipped out from under my arm. "Capture the flag!"

I tried to take the drink back and you slid down the bench, slapping my hands away.

Arturo walked up the path and joined us, carrying three more paper-bagged beers. We popped the cans open. Before the sky was even purple, streetlamps switched on.

Did I drink too much after that? Unemployed, with nothing to do the next day, did I decide to let go and stumble through the rest of the night? The evening is blank. After sunset, I don't remember anything.

.   .   .

By Monday, both of you were back at work, along with everyone else who hadn't fled El Cozon. I woke up late, grabbed my laptop off the nightstand, sat in bed, and looked through job boards. The city had returned to a nervous normal. Some offices had reopened. Some evacuees had returned. But hiring managers weren't advertising new positions. The little I could find—an archivist at an aerospace company, a research analyst at an entertainment conglomerate—had been posted before the mirror's appearance. The only new listing was an anonymous troll's joke, for a janitor at a company called The Sky. Its description read, "Keep reflection polished and gleaming. Qualifications: Proven ability to fly. Must provide own Windex."

With nothing to do, I went to the park, where the mirror kept me entertained through the long, dull day. Using binoculars, I examined curves that were too far away to see with the naked eye. Twisting and bending and reflecting off its own reflections, it showed street scenes and peered through windows. I saw a puppy steal a hot dog from a laughing little boy, an overconfident drunk girl trip over a curb, and a woman wave a young man into her corner office, close the door, and push him onto the desk. Hiking up her skirt, she jumped on top of his lap.

My binoculars went black. A woman stood in front of me, one hand clutching two plastic grocery bags full of used soda cans and plastic water bottles, the other raised to block my view of the mirror.

"Stop!" she said.

I tried to look around her open palm to see her face, but she kept her hand in front of my eyes. Thin lines of black grime caked the joints between her fingers.

"None of us asked to be watched by this thing."

Bringing her hand down, she revealed pale blue eyes and a wide forehead half-hidden behind locks of matted brown hair.

"Look around you, young man. No one else is staring at the sky."

Absorbed by the reflections, I hadn't noticed how the people in the park had changed. Everyone, from the walkers taking a shortcut home to the kids on the swings, avoided looking up. They didn't even raise their eyes to see the two squirrels chasing each other through the trees, noisily jumping from branch to branch.

"Stay out of other people's business." She angrily shook her bag of bottles, then turned and hobbled down the path.

.   .   .

A week later, Cassie, you texted me. "Bored. Leaving work. Where are u?" It was three in the afternoon, and I told you to come to my roof.

Looking through binoculars and laying my back, immersed in the mirror's world of reflected emotion, I didn't see you when you arrived.

"Is this where you were all day?"

A cool breeze blew, and I could smell you, the dusty drawers and bleached floors of the office where I used to work still clinging to your shirt. I sat up.

"Yeah. I can't go out in the street anymore. People get in my face."

Squinting, you examined me. "Of course they do."

"I don't get it. Why did everyone suddenly get so uptight about the mirror?"

"It's not too hard to get, guy."

"Explain it, then."

"People realized that, if they could look into other people's private lives, then those other people could look into their private lives. So most of us did the decent thing. We stopped looking."

I imagined someone on the other end of the city watching your reflection. With your back straight, a wide stretch of black tar between your feet and where I sat, it would have been clear to that theoretical watcher that this woman was unhappy with this man. I tried to explain why I didn't want to stop watching.

"I mean, everyone *says* they don't look. But they do. When they think no one is watching, they take a glimpse."

"That doesn't make it right."

"You see such amazing stuff, though."

"It's not for you to see, though," you said, mocking my intonation.

"The mirror's up there. We should all get used to it."

Taking a step back, you shook your head. "That's gross."

"Come on."

You turned around and left through the roof access door.

When I texted you later, your responses were short. I didn't know how to reply, so I put down my phone down and picked up my binoculars. A small propeller plane gained altitude. As it ascended, the mirror's surface flattened. For a few seconds, the plane flew directly beneath its own reflection. I could see its wheels and cockpit simultaneously as it floated below its upside-down copy. The real plane rose into the twin, absorbed itself, and disappeared. I waited for it to fly back out, to return from its trip into the mirror. Laying on the roof, I searched the sky.

.   .   .

Arturo, do you remember how hungover we were on the morning when Cassie came to work late, the day before I was fired? I sat next to you, sipping coffee and shaking, tremors running through my hands, afraid I would drop any exhibit I touched and shatter it on the floor.

Cassie, your eyes were red, and you avoided us, staying on the other side of the archive, ignoring our nonsensical, still half-drunk conversation. Only at lunch, when we went out and brought you back a super-sized cabeza burrito, did you break down and tell us that you had broken up with your boyfriend. Me and Arturo sat with you, at first cracking jokes we hoped would make you stop crying and smile, then quietly, my hand on your wrist, not knowing what to say.

We spent the afternoon discussing the wall the ancient city had built around itself halfway through its history. What was the best way to explain this sudden defensive frenzy? Up to that point, the city's construction had been entirely dedicated to elaborate ritual. Its streets ran east to west, aligned where the sun rose and set on the spring and fall equinox. Leaders lived on top of the steep earthen mounds. Their impractical homes had V-shaped inverted roofs that looked like they weren't made to shelter occupants but to hold up the sun.

Then, in a fit of defensive pragmatism, the city shut itself behind a two-mile wall. At seventy-yard intervals, they built guard towers that were solidly constructed at the base but tilted and twisted after they rose past heights the society's level of engineering could safely support.

The frantic construction expressed the emotion of panic, the feeling of fear, but the actual events that caused it were mysterious.

I picked through our collection of the culture's most common artistic artifacts, small ceramic figurines, each one crafted with precise flourishes, the only images we had of the individuals who spent their entire lives in the dead city. I wondered if I could find a way to make the sculptures tell the wall's story. Each had distinctive expressions, thick eyebrows or skinny legs, long hair or full lips, big shoulders or tiny waists, that communicated so much more detail than anything else the culture had left behind. The only thing the figurines had in common was their strange feet, always modeled after a bird's, with one long toe pointing forward, two to the sides, and a short claw at of the heel.

We discussed the issue long after our bosses left for the evening. I went out and brought back a fifth of whiskey. We passed it around, imagining increasingly absurd plans for the exhibition, making up stories about what had happened to these people, about the street sweeper's son who ran away with the king's daughter, about the architect who was buried under his shoddily made earthwork, about the boy who was swept out to sea when the river flooded then founded a new empire on the other side of the ocean.

The next morning was the first time I woke up in your

bed, Cassie. Putting on my pants, I found four figurines in my pocket, absent-mindedly taken out of the archive the night before, one broken in half, another smashed to dust.

. . .

Bored with the view from my roof, I went to a park between railroad tracks and a baseball stadium's parking lot, where a radio tower had been built on top of one of the earthworks. In an industrial part of town, it was avoided by anyone who would try to judge me for watching the mirror.

Hiking up a dirt path, I passed a tent with its door zipped shut. A woman slept in the shade of a rusted shopping cart filled with old clothes and yards of hand-spooled copper wire. Laundry draped over bushes. A dog ran happily to my feet, then darted away when an unseen owner called it back.

The fence around the lattice tower was topped with barbed wire, but its steel mesh had been cut away and torn back in dozens of places, making it easy to slip beneath. Dangling off a flat white-painted bar a few yards off the ground, his elbow wrapped around a corner beam, a lean man stared up at reflections. With his free hand, he scratched his arms through his thick cotton shirt, itching from his wrist to his bicep and back.

I climbed to a spot on the opposite side. As the sun set, rows of gray warehouse roofs turned purple. Above me, a teenager flicked his lighter in front of a body spray's nozzle, turning it into a DIY flame thrower. The fire caught on his greasy hair. He slapped his head to put it out, his friends fell down laughing, and I don't know what happened after that.

Time passed, an hour, maybe two, in blackness. I hadn't been drinking.

When I came to, I was looking at another curve in the sky, where a woman under a streetlamp's yellow light stared into the mirror even more intently than me. She wore a faded t-shirt. Dark hair fell to her shoulders. Her nose bent one centimeter to the right, her lips were parted, and her eyes were sad. The longer she looked up, the stiller she became, the more she focused on whatever it was she saw.

She was you, Cassie. Doing exactly what you had insulted me for doing on my own roof.

I climbed down and bent under the fence. The skinny man still clinging to the tower called out.

"Hey!"

I turned around.

"You like watching this thing?" Something about him looked pained. He shivered, as if a gust of January wind had blown through the summer night.

"Yeah."

"You might want to give it a rest." He scratched his arm fiercely. "Word to God, bro."

.   .   .

At home, I tried to distract myself with news about the sky. Searching my feeds, checking reporters' profiles, watching streams from local meteorologists who had become celebrities, I found nothing. I checked through it all again, rereading the same uninformative posts that had irritated me half a minute before. With phone in hand, too early to sleep, and thinking of you, I typed a message.

"I know you look at the mirror too."

Three dots popped up on-screen. I waited. Then, a one-character text. "?"

"I saw your reflection. You were watching the mirror. Today. An hour ago."

Again, three dots, no response. I swiped back to my feeds, reading without processing words.

Your message flashed blue. "It was my ex. I saw him up there."

I wrote back, "It's ok to spy when you spy on your ex-boyfriend. Cool."

"It wasn't right. But he looked so sad."

I didn't respond to that. You wrote the next text. "And I called him. We're talking again."

"Yeah. I get it."

"I'm sorry."

I put my cell face-down on my chest. Above my bed, the fire alarm's green light blinked. On and off. On and off. I counted seconds. The phone buzzed and I picked it up. "I like you. You're fun. But we weren't in love. We weren't going to fall in love."

The screen's light burned a white rectangle into my retina. The next text, the last text, was also from you. "Let's stay friends. That's what we always were."

I tried to think of ways to say I knew. Of course I did. We hung out together, we laughed, we drank, we woke up in the same bed, we went our separate ways, we did it again. I didn't love you. You didn't love me. But scattered through my empty days, those silly and superficial moments mattered.

As I fell asleep, talking to you in half-formed dreams, I scratched my arms. Clawing deeply, my nails dug into skin.

. . .

I woke up in the dark. You knocked on my bedroom door, Arturo.

"Yo."

Disoriented, I rolled over. "Huh?"

The only lights came from the blinking smoke detector and the glow of the streetlamps outside. You came in. "Why are you still sleeping?"

People talked on the sidewalk beneath my window. Their sentences were fast and clipped. Cars honked. It was too early to be so busy.

"What's going on?"

"You seen your phone, man?"

It was on the mattress next to me, screen black and battery dead. You showed me yours. An alert from the City of El Cozon, "MAYOR ORDERS EVACUATION."

"It woke me up fifteen minutes ago, squawking, screen flashing and everything." You switched on my bedside lamp. A backpack was slung over your shoulder, your boots were on, your hair was still bent sideways from being pressed against your pillow. "Mayor said the mirror is falling, DoD weather balloons clocked it a few hours ago. They had an emergency city council meeting and raised the red flag."

Kicking off blankets, I sat up.

"Your arms, dude. What's . . . " You gripped your backpack's strap tightly, eyebrows furrowed.

Lamplight bounced off my wrists. Blinking slowly, I raised them to my face. The spots glimmered. Clouded mirrors scabbed into me. I dug under a sliver and used my fingernails to peel it off. Beneath, the mirror wove deeper into my skin. I ripped another. More mirror. Fog obscured any image except for dull reflected light.

"Man . . ." You pulled the backpack's second strap over your shoulder. "We gotta go."

"But . . ."

"See a doctor after we're out of here. I don't want to know what happens when this thing hits our heads."

I blacked out.

■　■　■

My hand was wrapped around a man's strong wrist. A crowd pressed against us. He turned to me, confused.

"What's wrong?"

He had broad dark cheeks and wore a backpack over his slim shoulders. It was you, Arturo.

"Where are we?"

"What?" You shook your wrist out of my grip. "Are you okay?"

I looked around. We stood in a quiet mob waiting to walk up a railway platform.

"I don't remember how we got here." I felt myself stooping over, hiding beneath the crowd.

For a moment, your lips parted but didn't respond. Putting your hand in your pocket, you shielded the wrist I had grabbed. "Don't worry. It's probably just the rush of all this." You glanced at the sky. "PTSD or something. We'll go to a doctor when we're out of here."

"It's not just this morning. I blacked out yesterday. Maybe before then, too." I leaned in closer to you, to the strength of your straight-backed posture.

"Okay, okay. Calm down." You slipped an unconscious half-inch away from me. "But listen. Until we see that doctor, don't touch anyone. That shit in your arms could be infectious."

As the mirror went from night's black to the dark blue before dawn, no one around us pushed. We watched trains run down the track, stop at the station, and continue on. Through carriage windows, we could see that they were already full by the time they arrived.

It didn't look like the mirror was less high than it had been the day before. The only difference was the number of helicopters that flew above us, hospitals carrying patients away, police hovering.

My arms itched. Holding them close to my sides, I resisted the urge to scratch.

A train came down the track. It was only half full. As it braked, inertia made passengers holding straps lean forward. Unlike people in the earlier trains, they weren't held stiffly upright by masses of evacuees crammed together.

The street's crowd surged toward the staircase, the tide splitting couples apart. Fathers shouted children's names. A woman was knocked between us, Arturo. She slowly lost her balance, tipping toward the pavement.

"Stop!"

"Wait!"

Men spread their legs and stood their ground, pushing back against the pressure. Women told their neighbors to be patient. The street calmed. Crouching, I helped the woman to her feet and tried to reach through legs for her sunglasses that had fallen off. She said, "Never mind. They're not important."

A little boy, maybe five years old, passed over people's heads, from one set of arms to another, until he reached the mother who yelled, "Over here! Over here!" Panic subsided. We waited patiently, letting tired neighbors lean against us.

Dawn's yellow bent across the mirror as a sharp pain shot through my arms. Without thinking, I pulled my sleeve up. The fog on my scabbed wrist had cleared. In its reflection, we appeared. You, Cassie. You, Arturo. Me. Not by the train station but in the museum's windowless archive, months before, passing a fifth of whiskey around the table, pottery and clay figurines spread in front of us.

I pulled my sleeve up further. On another scab, you and I sat on a bench, Cassie. Next to us, three boys ate popsicles and stuck out their tongues. The scab under that one showed me and Arturo in the back of a dark bar, where no windows looked out to the street, drunkenly toasting to our first day as curatorial assistants.

These weren't only moments that could have been seen from the sky. They weren't only times when the mirror had been above us. My scabs showed rooms deep in basements, long before the reflection had emerged. It was everything. Every moment we spent together, every detail of every night we stumbled from bar to bar, every second we worked side-by-side.

The world I loved was fading, my city evacuating, my memory disappearing, Cassie gone. Except here. Stored in these mirrors.

"Are those—recordings?" Arturo, you recoiled. "Holy shit."

The tall woman pressed against my other shoulder took a forceful step back, looking at the mirrors and spreading her arms to push people away from me.

Rolling my sleeves down, I retreated, walking out of the crowd.

"Watch out!" "Don't touch him!"

. . .

Maybe the mirror is sentient. Maybe it was created by something sentient. I don't know. Intentionally or not, it revealed itself to me.

Avoiding the evacuation order was easy. The police had an entire city to search and focused on rescue, not forced removal. From the safety of my roof, I peered into the street and watched them run into apartment buildings, inside each no longer than ten minutes. When I heard them break through my building's front door, I shut myself in a closet. Dashing from room to room, boots stomping heavily, they shouted, "Anyone here?" I sat in the dark and ate a half-finished can of cold chicken soup.

Every day, the mirror fell faster. I think. I don't remember much.

When I look in the kitchen, I see that almost all the cans of soup are gone. No one else is here. I must have eaten them myself.

This morning, the skyscrapers' roofs disappear. Instead of a top story, they have two bottom floors, one on earth's ground, the other on the ground reflected in the sky. Between the two, buildings stretch uninterrupted. They've become bridges.

Before I walk up, I want to tell you, Arturo, and you, Cassie, what I'll bring back. As I've waited for the mirror to fall, the only hours I haven't lost are the ones I spent looking at my arms, being with you again. I saw you, Cassie, acting out the story of the buried architect on the night we imagined how people in the dead city had lived. I saw you, Arturo, pick up the purses, keys, and hats I and Cassie would always absentmindedly leave behind. It's so easy to forget little things.

I believe all of it is up there. Every minute. Every detail. It's stored in the mirror. If I bring it back, we can hold onto it forever.

And if the mirror won't release what it has absorbed, then this story is for you. Give it to your children and nieces and nephews and grandchildren, to all of the people who never knew us when we were young, to the future that will never know our city. The past will always be here.

BOILING POINT

Samuel Clark

BOILING POINT

Samuel Clark

My mother lived in a house of cake and so did I.

She'd pick at its walls, chocolate sponge, while I sat at her table, a plate of crayfish shells for supper. She wanted me skinny, would count my ribs instead of sheep, while I read stories of witches and fattening, boys made plump for the oven, and dream of a life outside her walls.

I learned quickly what it meant to eat the house, to eat anything without her knowledge. On the day she caught me licking a window—its glass made entirely of sugar—she broke every pane in the cottage. "How am I to know which ones you infected with that greedy little tongue?" It was my job to rebuild. My punishment. I was to bake every new window, a painstaking process, the smell of warm sugar just inches away as I measured and poured. My mother kept watch, assuring no morsel met my tongue until the job was finished.

It took me over a week.

Skinnier and skinnier and skinnier—hunger pangs and waning attention, dizzy spells and weakening—but I could not stop reading them, the fairy tales. The promise of something outside my mother's control. It was not their happy endings that inspired want in me—I was too acquainted with life for that, knew better than to hope for true love and ever afters—but the food. The food! Hunks of bread and rounds of cheese. Ale and apples, figs and pots of butter. Sausages. Wine. Golden eggs and honey. Plums, pears, porridge and pomegranates. Lembas wrapped in Mallorn leaves. Roast goose. On every page, a lost boy, a child whose crime was hunger. I saw myself in them, and beyond that, a dining hall, a table filled with the foods of our choosing, the lost boys and I, seated together at last.

This is all to say you must forgive me. Or at the very least, try to understand.

It was a cold night, the temperature below freezing, and I had been sent out to fetch kindling for the woodstove. The wind tore through my skin, chapped and cracking, and I thought of my mother back home, wrapped in down feathers and wool.

Done with my errand, I returned with the wheelbarrow in tow, the top brimming over with pine. My mother sat at the kitchen table, where she dipped fresh bread into potato soup, the steam still rising from the bowl. The sight made me salivate, lost in a haze of hungry want.

"Are you going to stand there or build us a fire?"

Wordlessly I turned to the stove, filling its belly with wood, while I prayed my mother would allow me a portion once I completed the task at hand. Being careful not to stop what I was doing, I stood on my toes to peer into the pot of soup, shoving a new handful of kindling into the stove's iron mouth as I did so.

Empty.

Behind me, my mother licked and chomped, licked and chomped. It was the loudest sound in the world.

A rogue flame leapt from the woodstove, nipping the

end of my finger. I yelped, an instinctive response, before sticking the offended tip into my mouth, sucking at the pain as though it were venom.

My mother stood from the table, visibly annoyed. "Move," she said and shoved me out of the way.

You've read the stories too, haven't you? You know what happens next.

Her back to me, I watched as she stoked the fire, cursing my name between handfuls of lumber, the smell of our house so sweet and so good. The perfume of chocolate, our walls growing warm with sugar, the windows humming at their hinges as the snow fell and fell and fell.

I pressed my hand into her back and pushed.

It was easy.

From behind the iron door of the stove, she called to me. Begged. I didn't taunt her. I didn't do much of anything. I was too tired, too hungry for games. Instead, I sat on the hearth and waited, my stomach growling at the promise of meat.

SELECTIONS FROM THE DEWEY DECIMAL

Cassidy McFadzean

SELECTIONS FROM THE DEWEY DECIMAL

Cassidy McFadzean

001 KNOWLEDGE; 021 LIBRARY RELATIONSHIPS; 098 PROHIBITED WORKS, FORGERIES, HOAXES

My first memory of the library was locking myself in it. I remembered pushing the door, and then pulling on it, and then when it wouldn't open, fiddling with the lock until a woman made her way down the stairs and opened it for me. In my memory, the woman sighed. She was a tall, Indigenous woman in a blazer and dark wash jeans. She might have been my supervisor, Sandra, who ten years later hired me to work as a clerk. Ten years ago, I would have been twelve, and still capable of locking myself inside unfamiliar buildings.

"Next year is the centennial," Sandra said, as she toured me the staff room, the bathroom, the boiler room. "We're a hundred years old, and finally moving into the mâmawâyâwin center."

She took me up to the front desk where a dark-haired girl a few years older than me was seated behind the counter, chewing gum, and texting on her phone. She introduced herself as Tanis, "the pregnant chick" in my brother's year, but I didn't remember her.

"No running on the stair!" she called to the group of kids she'd given computer passes. "It's all yours," she said, sliding off the stool.

I stood at Sandra's side as she distributed holds to waiting patrons, checked out books, and conducted searches on the computer, all the while narrating her actions.

"Are you following all this?" she asked, demonstrating the process for signing up a new patron. I copied her last few instructions into my notebook and practiced making a profile while she took a phone call in the back.

When I looked up, an old woman stood at the front desk. She was dressed in layers of wool and thin gauzy scarves wrapped around her which was how I finally recognized her as the old woman who lived down the block from my parents' house. She spent her days sweeping leaves out of the storm drains and my mom said hello whenever we passed. The woman looked past me to Sandra stirring a mug of coffee, waving her clipping of *NYT* bestsellers and calling her back to the counter. A mess of ballpoint ink and orange highlighter filled the margins of the newsprint, but Sandra discerned the order behind the tightly looped cursive.

"Do you have this book?" she pointed with her yellowed fingernail.

Sandra typed on the keyboard and said we didn't have the title at our branch, but she could place it on hold. Alongside my notes, I listed each of the patterns the old woman wore: floral, paisley, leopard, zebra, a menagerie of prints.

"That's fine," she said, and passed her card across the desk. She leaned over the counter. "What about this title? What is your opinion? I don't wish to read anything obscene."

"Oh," Sandra said, and laughed. "I have to admit I was curious, and I did read it. I can tell you that it is erotic, but at the same time it is quite popular with many of our patrons."

"I don't know about that," the woman said.

"It deals with themes of submission. Some women find it appealing."

"Well, you might as well place it on hold," she said.

"Alrighty then," Sandra said, and typed into the catalogue.

When the old woman made her way down the stairs and exited the building, Tanis returned for another pile of magazines.

"Why are white people so crazy?" she asked. "She comes in here smelling like booze at ten AM. What's so bad that you have to drink as soon as you wake up?"

I shrugged, not wanting to share that I'd known her from the time I was a little girl, that she'd once passed a tightly bound bouquet of her petunias over the fence of her garden.

110 METAPHYSICS; 158 APPLIED PSYCHOLOGY; 177 ETHICS OF SOCIAL RELATIONS

To familiarize myself with the catalogue, Sandra had me go through the rows of children's books, putting them back in order. As I worked through the picture books and youth non-fiction, I had to clean the hardened gum, sunflower seed shells, old pennies, and chip bags that were lodged between shelves containing books on puberty and healthy eating. I cleaned a handful of pencil shavings from the corner of a shelf and scooped a napkin of seeds out from under *Your Changing Body* and into the trash bin.

When I moved to the low shelves of board books, I smelled the soiled diaper of a young girl leaning over a Lego set. "Her mom's outside having a smoke," Tanis called over. "These parents don't look after their kids. Once I asked a little boy what he'd do if we closed, and he said he'd just run around outside."

I knew there was more to the situation than Tanis suggested, but it wasn't my place to say so. I returned to the shelves where, lodged between two animal books, I found a puzzle piece in the shape of a boy's arm. The puzzle was difficult for most kids because instead of a single sheet, it had to be completed in sections. Its layered pieces represented the different components of the human body: the first a boy's transparent organs, then his skeleton with white bones, his red muscles and veins, his naked flesh (complete with an oval for his penis), and finally his clothes and ball cap. You had to lay down the pieces layer by layer to successfully put the body together. I placed the wooden limb back on its body and picked up an old sock next to the puppets scattered on the floor. "Anyone lose a sock?" I said to no response.

"Everyone, this is Katie," Tanis shouted. "She's new, but she's cool. Listen to her, okay?"

I slid the sock over my hand and had the sock repeat the question in the first person. I thought the kids would laugh but they just stared at me until I stood up.

"Just put it in the lost and found," Tanis said.

I joined her behind the desk and began sorting a stack of horror movies and pow-wow DVDs we kept behind the desk.

211 CONCEPTS OF GOD; 216 NO LONGER USED— FORMERLY EVIL; 269 SPIRITUAL RENEWAL

I was working alone for the first time while Sandra was downstairs in her office and Tanis was on her lunch break. Her mother was sick, and she sometimes left early to take her to doctor appointments or disappeared on her breaks. A woman stood at the front desk dressed in an ill-fitting dress shirt and wool skirt. She asked for a tape by a comedian I remembered watching in high school Cree class.

"We do have a few copies, but they're all out at the moment," I said, doing my best to imitate Sandra.

"Oh no, that's too bad. Can I put a hold on them?"

I clicked on the listing. "I guess they're actually lost," I said. "Sorry."

I should have noticed this detail first and was reminded of an earlier incident when I had a patron drive across town for *Laurence of Arabia* when we only had the disc of special features.

"Laughter is good therapy," the woman said. "You know, I counsel all sorts of women, and I believe that laughter is one way to speak those tears. Once you get one woman laughing, they'll all start laughing. One starts crying, and they all start crying. It's because all women have suffered in one way or another, and we recognize it in one another."

"I guess so," I said. There was no one waiting in line, and so the woman felt no pressure to leave.

"Every pain is localized in a different area. If you have a pain in your back, it means you're being self-righteous. Pain in your heel, and you need to stand your ground."

"What about a pain in your neck?"

"Judgmental. What you speak out comes right back to you. The devil didn't do this to you. You did this to you. People who say they don't want to be like that—that's what they become. You name your fears. You get what you speak. It all comes back to you. And I've been there. I've lived it all. It's all in my past. I used to be like that too, self-righteous. Every sickness you cause yourself."

"Really? That seems a bit like blaming the victim."

"How old are you, sweetie?" the woman asked.

"Twenty-two. But don't you think there's just evil people in the world? Things that just happen for no reason?"

"You know, my mother has rheumatoid arthritis. Her sister broke her back in residential schools. They threw her down the stairs. She held onto that anger and hatred all these years and now she's dying of it. If she had only learned to forgive . . . "

"I don't see, medically speaking, how anger causes arthritis."

"Medically speaking, the body and mind are connected," she said. "Like how I can see my words are upsetting you."

"I can write down your name and let you know if the CD comes back," I said.

"Certainly. My name is Mary." She passed me a faded library card. "It's an old-fashioned name. A Catholic name. A lot of Marys back in the residential school days."

I scanned her card and made a note in her file.

"You know," Mary continued. "I've been around a long time, and a lot of people think I'm crazy, but I don't care what they say."

"I don't think anything."

Mary gestured to her chest, and tapped the skin

exposed above her shirt's top button.

"You have a knot of pain right here," she said. "I can see it clear as day."

I turned and hid in the back room, where I heard Mary slowly making her way down the stairs. I filled the kettle, and when I returned to the front desk, Mary was gone but Sandra was in her place, adjusting the piles of bookmarks.

"Please don't leave the front desk if you're the only up here."

"Right," I said. "Sorry."

307 COMMUNITIES; 326 SLAVERY & EMANCIPATION; 362 SOCIAL PROBLEMS & SERVICES

I flipped the open sign and unlocked the door of the library. The weight of the deadbolt clicked out of the steel frame, and a group of kids in rushed inside. Their hair was white with flurries, their cheeks bright red from waiting in the wind. I taped up a poster advertising the community feast the library was hosting the next month.

I said hello to an older man who entered the library. He was wearing a leather jacket and immediately headed for the children's section, where he sat on a tiny plastic chair. Tanis raised her brow. "Just watch him," she said in a lowered voice. "We get some creeps in here. It's not illegal to watch porn, unless it's child porn. And then we have to catch them in the act."

The possibility was so terrifying, I pretended I didn't hear. I glanced up and the man moved from the chair to the computer. I went in the back room and placed a teabag in a cup of lukewarm water. When I came back out, Tanis was flipping through a magazine, ignoring the man in the leather jacket, now standing at the desk.

"Can I get some help?" he asked.

"Sure," I said, and followed him over to the computer, nervous at what I might find. Some kid had already dismantled the anatomy puzzle, and I stepped over the transparent lungs and arms scattered on the floor.

"I can't seem to delete this," the man said. I glanced at the screen. It showed a registry of Jewish citizens. He was trying to find his family, to learn more about himself. Maybe he had lost relatives in the holocaust. Maybe his grandparents had met in a camp.

I showed him how to highlight and delete his search phrase, and how to enter a new one. He thanked me, and I returned to the front desk, where I told Tanis the man was only researching his family tree.

"Some people are for real crazy though," she said. "We had a woman in here wearing only a bra and skirt with no shoes. Sandra had to tell her to go home and put some shoes on. She comes in with seriously every pair of shoes she owns and dumps them on the counter. *Is that enough shoes for you*, she says. We just look at her and start laughing. She lives across the street and calls the main office if we close early. Wicked alcoholic, comes in here smelling like booze. I think she's on her meds now though. I haven't seen her in a while."

I left the desk to shelve a stack of books Tanis had let pile up the night before. I focused on sorting the spines to their position on the shelves and tried to calm my breathing. When I returned for another stack, Tanis was stirring a cup of hot chocolate.

"You know, you remind me of my brother," she said. "Me and my brother are twins, but he grew up with my Auntie in Saskatoon when I had to stay here."

"I grew up here too," I said.

"I know, but my brother, he had a good life. He didn't have to deal with anything like I did. My mom's drinking. Nothing."

"I'm sorry," I said.

"It's whatever," she said, flipping through the stack of posters. "Have you ever even been to a feast before?"

"Just the ones at school."

"I meant a real one," she said.

403 DICTIONARIES, ENCYCLOPEDIAS, CONCORDANCES; 411 WRITING SYSTEMS; 497 NORTH AMERICAN NATIVE LANGUAGES

Sandra asked if I ever filled up one of my notebooks, so I lied and said no, and told her it was just for grocery lists, or keeping track of books I wanted to read. She nodded, but didn't seem convinced and after that, I left my notebook in my bag.

"I'm out, bitches," Tanis announced. Her boyfriend, a broad-shouldered man who towered over her, stood at the door with sunglasses and his arms crossed. She held to the arm of his hoodie, and they left, walking down the middle of the avenue.

I turned to the cart of books Tanis had let fill up. She would have complained if I'd done the same, but I welcomed the chance to leave the front desk, even if the pile was mainly the Indigenous Voices Collection our branch specialized in—there were so many books with 970, and 971 call numbers that it was difficult to keep them straight. Often, only one digit or letter varied, and I had to scan the shelves repeatedly just to place a single book. I'd already begun to let the North American History fall into disarray.

As I carried my first heavy pile into the adult section, an elderly woman entered the library. "I'm just here to read," the woman said, smiling at me when I greeted her. She sat on the vinyl chairs near the magazines and opened the Saturday paper. I set down the pile and returned the books to the shelves, where I found a stack that had been left on the floor. The woman's cell phone rang, resounding in the otherwise quiet room. She answered and began speaking in Cree. The lulling rhythm of her voice, familiar from childhood, brought me out of myself. I hadn't heard those sounds since high school, and I could no longer discern their meaning. They were equally distant and immediate. Even after the woman finished the call, my stomach sunk with the feeling that something was out of place, and it was me.

I took another pile of books and CDs into the next room. I scanned their barcodes, found their right place in the right shelf, and slid them into place. I straightened the spines of the books, so the shelves were smooth. My third pile of books took me to the corner of the non-fiction section, where a girl with blue-streaked hair was seated on the floor, her head bent over a textbook. I thought she might have been a former classmate, but her hair was hanging over her face and I couldn't tell for sure.

I returned to the front desk for more books, and Sandra sent me down to the basement to get some of the Halloween books we kept in storage. When I came back upstairs, the girl was gone, and a computer search of recent patrons only brought up a picture of Mary. Her eyes were narrowed as if she were staring right into me. I closed the computer window and sized up the pile of books I still had to put away. One had been stained with coffee and its pages had become brown and crinkled. I placed it on a shelf for Sandra to examine with the other titles removed from circulation, their covers ripped off, spines damaged, awaiting the year-end used book sale or the recycling bin.

520 ASTRONOMY; 535 LIGHT AND RELATED RADIATION; 586 CRYPTOGAMIA (SEEDLESS PLANTS)

I came in early on Saturday to clean the counters, vacuum the keyboards, and water the plants. Somehow, I'd begun watering the plastic plants. At first, it had been an accident. I'd noticed a dust-covered tree in the corner of the computer lab and poured a Big Gulp of tap water into the planter. After that, I'd started doing it on purpose. It was a small act of resistance, like the times I let patrons use the phone when Sandra forbade it. Or when I forgave a girl's fines who wanted to read *April Raintree*. I let teenagers check out DVDs rated R and 18A and overrode their holds. I made restrictions disappear. I replaced cards free of charge. Now I stared at the plastic plants floating in their pots. The water would disappear by my next shift.

When I came upstairs, Tanis still hadn't arrived. I continued my chores, cleaning the phones and screens with Lysol wipes, checking to see if she'd left a message. When these tasks were finished, I started sorting the holds and returns. Finally, at five minutes before one, Tanis came in the front doors. I went downstairs to use the washroom and when I came up, she was leaning over the counter and talking to Mary, who had materialized with an unnerving punctuality. I went in the back and began sorting the supply drawer.

"She's been seeing things. It's not a good sign," Tanis said in a quiet voice. "It's how my Auntie was before she died."

"What kind of things?" Mary said.

"She saw a man in her garden, in the backyard behind the house. She started yelling at me, telling me to search the yard. She was so convinced someone was there. She made me lock the gate, but the gate was already locked."

"I see," Mary said.

"Well her surgery is coming up. Hopefully it helps. Like, she thought the man was stealing her potatoes, digging them up. She didn't even plant any potatoes this year."

"These presences, they can mean she's nearing the end," Mary said. "When the worlds start to veer together in this way."

Then Mary said something in a quiet voice I couldn't hear, and I went out to the front desk, feeling around in my back pocket for a scrap of paper and my pen.

"What are you looking for?" Tanis said.

"Tape."

She handed me a roll of tape from the tape drawer.

"Thanks." I said. I crouched behind the desk, straightening the hold shelf. When Mary finally left, Tanis went in the back to argue with her boyfriend on the phone as she counted the coins from the cash register. I sorted the rest of the mail. *Residential Schools in Canada; The Indian Act and Residential Schools*. I shelved the heavy volumes and emptied the crate of books.

"That fucking asshole!" Tanis called out from the next room.

646 SEWING, CLOTHING; 685 LEATHER & FUR GOODS; 698 DETAIL FINISHING

Sandra had me cutting leather into patterns for the kid's afterschool program. My scissors sliced through the thick fabric, leaving brown shavings on my jeans. While I cut the leather, Tanis signed up kids for the computer lab.

"I'm waiting for you to say something," Tanis said to one kid at the counter as she read the page of horoscopes. "I'm not going to help you until you think of what it is."

"Please and thank you can I use the computer?" the little boy said.

"That's better. We're full. You'll have to wait an hour."

The little boy left the counter, and a skinny white guy approached us next.

"Can I get some help?" he asked. He was a mainstay in the computer lab, and I'd once glanced at his screen to discover all his emails were avowals of love to one woman, his messages never returned.

Tanis looked at me, and so I placed the bag of moccasin patterns on the counter and followed him down into the basement. I heard Sandra talking on the telephone in her office as the boiler hissed, obscuring her voice. In the lab, the children crouched up on their seats, and two or three leaned over the same screen. "It's broken," the man said, motioning to his screen.

The monitor was black, so I wiggled the mouse and pressed a few random keys. I glanced at the tower below the desk and saw a loose cord. "It's not plugged in."

The man continued staring at me. Then I understood: he wanted me to get on my knees and plug in the computer for him. I turned from him without saying anything and headed back up the stairs. When I passed Sandra's office, her door was closed.

"Please and thank you. Can I sign up?" a little boy said to Tanis.

"You've already been down so no," Tanis said, sending the boy away.

"I think we should watch that guy down there," I said, pulling the logbook.

"He seemed like a perv," she said. "You writing him up?

"Just seeing if there's anything on him already."

"I can tell him it's for kids only," she offered. "I do that sometimes if I get a bad vibe."

"Definitely for the best," I said. "It's about safety after all."

727 BUILDINGS FOR EDUCATIONAL & RESEARCH PURPOSES; 753 SYMBOLISM, ALLEGORY, MYTHOLOGY, LEGEND; 793 INDOOR GAMES AND AMUSEMENTS

Tanis was waiting for a cab outside with her boyfriend and kids—one dressed as a witch, one a princess, and the boy in a Jason mask. Their pillowcases were already heavy with candy Tanis had scooped from the library's plastic pumpkin dish and into their bags.

A woman and her two kids entered the library as Sandra gushed over their costumes.

"Can you say trick-or-treat?" I asked the children.

"This one doesn't talk," the woman said, resting her hand on the older one's shoulder. "This one does."

"Well, can you say trick-or-treat?" I asked the older one.

"Trick-or-treat," the girl said in a quiet voice. I gave

them a handful of candy each.

In a few minutes, the face painters arrived. The man had a gold glint to his teeth, and the woman's face was painted like a sugar skull. They spoke Spanish to each other as they set up their station on the children's tables. They spread out their paints and sponges, while Sandra poured water in buckets for them to use.

A couple kids entered the library and I watched as the woman covered the little boy's face with white paint, and the man shaded his features into a skull, hollowing his eyes, and making his cheeks and nose appear sunken. When they'd finished his face, they turned to his brother. The boys grinned at their reflections. I watched the skull children change places with a group of plain-clothed kids, their faces clean. They left out the front door, transformed into skeletal versions of themselves.

I heard yelling from outside and followed Sandra to the door. On the front steps of the library, Tanis' boyfriend was bleeding on the ground. A large man loomed over him, pounding his face as Tanis tried to pull the man away. Sandra was already on the phone with the police, and I led Tanis's kids back inside the library.

"Stop it!" Tanis screamed. She pulled at the man's hair, and he loosened his grip on her boyfriend. Tanis pulled him up from the ground and she ran inside the door. Her boyfriend kicked the other man, which gave him enough time to open the door of the library and join her inside. His white jacket was covered in blood from his nose and face, and Sandra pulled the kids aside while Tanis struggled to lock the door. The man lurched it open, pounding on the glass, but Tanis called out that the cops were on their way and slammed the door shut. She turned the deadbolt in the frame, and her boyfriend wiped his face on his jacket.

819 NO LONGER USED—FORMERLY PUZZLE ACTIVITIES; 826 ENGLISH LETTERS; 890 OTHER LITERATURES

I stared at the poster in the lobby. It featured a photograph of Mary prominently displayed. *Spiritual Yoga* it read. *Weekly replenishment for the soul.* Sign-up information ran along the bottom of the poster. The program had already filled up, and there were talks of Mary offering an additional section in the spring.

With five minutes left in my shift, an old white man approached the counter.

"Excuse me," he said. "Can I get some help copying these?" I put his change in the photocopier and glanced to the first page of the man's document: "To Whom it Does Concern."

"I'll give you a history lesson, how about that?" the man said. "My last name is Chideock. My descendants were saints and smugglers. You see this family tree—" he showed me the next sheet. "I'm a direct descendent of King Henry the Seventh and Queen Elizabeth. Back in the day, Catholicism was illegal, and so my ancestors were smugglers. Smugglers and Saints. Maybe now I'll get my God-damned citizenship. You know if you fill out one form incorrectly, they'll make you do it all over again and keep your money."

"I heard it's difficult."

"Well, here's the next sheet," the man said. "History of Chideock."

"You want four copies of each?"

"Just one of that. That's just for me."

"Okay," I said, and fed the paper into the machine.

"I appreciate your help. I have to convince them when I'm a direct descendant. It's here on the paper. I can't make it any clearer."

"Well, good luck."

I returned to the front desk and gathered my coat and backpack from beneath the counter and hollered to Tanis that I was taking off. Outside, kids were playing in the snowbank. I passed the poppy-red stain in the snow, and when I looked back, one of the kids was helping a woman carry her stroller up the stairs.

913 ANCIENT WORLD; 991–992 NOT ASSIGNED OR NO LONGER USED; 999 EXTRATERRESTRIAL WORLDS

"C'mon," Tanis said. "It's time."

"I'm not sure I should," I said. "Maybe next year."

"Just come," she said. "We need more women."

I followed Tanis into the program room in the basement. The children were already seated along the walls: the boys on one side of the room, and the girls on the other side. I sat with Tanis and Sandra beside the elder. Across the wall, I saw Mary, and the others from the area. The teenage girls and their younger siblings. Tanis's kids were playing with paper dolls they'd made in school that day. On my left, there were the older men from the language programs, those who came to read the newspaper each day or use the computers. The elder's helper burned the sage and blessed the colored cloths. In the center of the room, there were pots of soup and trays of bannock. I glanced at the boxes of apples, and bananas and oranges, and salmon and grease, and Saskatoon berries.

I sat on the floor in a borrowed skirt, listening as the elder told a story that could only be told while there was snow on the ground, a story that could not be repeated.

I closed my eyes when he began to pray. He spoke in a deep voice the words of my childhood. He prayed in a rhythmic lull that sounded like poetry. He was praying for the health and safety of all in the community. He smudged with the pipe and smoked the tobacco. He gave an offering of grease and soup and tobacco to the spirits. It was a gift in return for the blessing. He asked for peace for the community's residents. The room filled with the smoke and smell of sage and sweet grass. The men passed the pipe and smoked from it, or just held it to their hearts. The helpers poured the soup into the bowls and began moving clockwise around the room, handing out the food.

Then I heard a drumming at the window, and children's faces pressed against the glass, and I left the circle to let them in.

THE WINNERS

Lori Sambol Brody

THE WINNERS

Lori Sambol Brody

It's Aaron's idea to enter the contest to win a weekend in an Eastern European castle. *It'll be fun,* he says. *Castle B— has a mirror maze and a resident ghost, the Red Lady.* I ask about bathrooms, central heating. *Why are you such a spoilsport?* He leans close as if he's confiding a secret. *I'll write an article about it.* I know I'll be in that article, rendered thin as paper; I'll have some crisis he invents to manufacture conflict. He clicks through websites in foreign languages, shows me pixelated photographs of dark shapes I can only identify by not looking directly at them, like glimpsing dim stars through a telescope. *You are not endearing me to this castle,* I say. He savagely shuts his laptop. *You can work on your poetry collection,* he says. A cheap shot, the manuscript gathering dust.

What is the chance of his winning? One in ten thousand? *OK fine,* I say.

I am nothing but the supportive wife.

Six months later. We barely talking (my fault). A plane to an Eastern European capital, another plane to a university city in the north, where the protests occurred two years ago, a taxi (Russian model, bungees securing the rear bumper) racing on serpentine mountain roads through villages squatting in gorges, the driver's arm thrown across the back of the passenger seat (dark rabbit-shaped mole on the hairy back of his hand), and, finally, our destination: iron gates open and the taxi's tires crunch on a dirt driveway. Castle B— is composed of the requisite dark granite, soaring battlements, red-tiled roof, and turrets. The building looms, it hunches, it throws dark shadows on what remains of the castle's park, the windblown twisted trees, dark winding paths.

A crone (as Aaron calls her later) guides us up steep narrow stone steps with surprising alacrity, never using her cane tipped with bone. Her hair is dyed pale lavender to hide the grey, her month pursed. On the back of her hand, a mole in the shape of a rabbit. She opens a heavy wood door. *Our bedroom suite,* she annunciates in perfect English. White-washed walls, four-poster bed hung with forest green velvet curtains, a chandelier of antlers. A stove covered with porcelain tile commands one wall.

My wife is concerned about bathrooms, Aaron says. I have said nothing of the sort since he won the contest. The crone opens a door, gestures with her cane at the Jacuzzi tub, moss-colored towels on a chrome towel heater, the gleaming white toilet with mysterious buttons. She tells us the cook left us a hot meal in the kitchen and will return at eight in the morning for breakfast, then will leave lunch and dinner in the refrigerator. The crone points to a thick notebook with a drawing of a woman and the words "Manual of Castle B—" on the cover. *This is everything you need to know. How to work that for heat—* another gesture with her cane to the tile stove. She shoves a laminated paper at us: a map of Castle B—, the writing blurry and indistinct, the lamination yellow and peeling at the corners.

Go with god, she says, giving us the typical farewell of the country, at least as per Aaron. *Beware of the Red Lady.* And then shuts the creaking door of the bedroom suite behind her.

She plays her part well, he says. *Good thing we don't believe in ghosts.* He sits on the mattress, bounces a little. *This will be great for my back. Better than our sofa.* I guess he's decided to share a bed again. I roll my suitcase into a corner, start unpacking into the drawers of a heavy dark dresser. Sweaters and T-shirt in this drawer. Underwear here, a set of the nice lacy stuff, just in case.

Aaron tosses the Manual at me. The drawing on the cover reminds me of a Renaissance painting: a woman crowned with a red cloth headdress and dressed in a red robe with long bell sleeves. In handwriting, someone has written (in an attempt at iambic poetry): *She appears to the guilty and the curséd / She appears to the holy and the blesséd.*

Oh, thanks, I say. Holding the manual in my hands as if I'm actually going to read it.

You can figure out how the stove works. It'll get even colder at night.

The stove's huge; a niche beside it holds logs cut almost exactly the same size. A small metal door to put the logs in. *It's pretty self-explanatory.*

My eyes keep returning to the stove, even if I look away, as if the stove compels me to regard it as the center of my existence. The tiles are painted in faded colors with hunting scenes. Hunters and their dogs pursue a white stag, the stag rests with its head on a maiden's lap, the maiden, like the woman on the Manual, is dressed all in red and protects the stag from the hunters. The nostrils of the stag flare as it breathes. I mean: as if I watch a movie, the nostrils expand, the maiden's veil blows in a breeze, a hunter throws his spear to strike the maiden, and the maiden writhes in widening pool of blood.

And then the images are still.

Aaron waves the map in front of my face. *Earth to Lucy*, he says. *Let's explore.*

I must have been hallucinating due to fatigue and jet lag. *I need a nap.*

Suit yourself.

In the space between our words, an electrified hum pulses, power being delivered to the light bulbs through the walls. He leaves and the bed is perfect for *my* back. I dream of trapdoors opening into dungeons and a woman all in red and corridor walls moving to trap me. When I awake, Aaron tells me about his explorations. What you would expect: dark corners, winding staircases, locked doors.

In the kitchen, at a long, scarred table, we eat dumplings, thinly sliced beef with a syrupy red sauce, and a hazelnut and raspberry torte. The crone left us a bottle of local wine as heavy as fresh blood: on the bottle, silver writing, *Welcome to the Winners*. Aaron takes my hand. Kisses my life line. *I have forgiven you*, he says, *I want to work on our marriage*, he says. In the corner, a mouse convulses from rodenticide. My palms sweat from the heat of the kitchen. *Show me the castle*, I say.

Tomorrow. He leads me to the curtained bed, covers my mouth with his. Rain lashes the windows.

In the morning he's already typing on his laptop, drinking tea. Writing that article, I assume. I spiral down the stairs to the kitchen.

The cook is a twin to the crone, flowered kerchief on her lavender hair, the same rabbit-shaped mole. Are all of them siblings, the taxi driver, the crone, and the cook?

Or the same person, disguised in different clothes and wigs? She also wields a cane, the handle carved into stag's horns. *Let me help you,* I say, but she makes me sit at the table and sets before me eggs with bold orange yolks and shot after shot of the coffee they make in this country, thick and black and sweet. She repeats the word *charveney,* insistent, then points to a red dish towel, and I realize she means the color red. I shake my head *I don't understand,* and she makes the sign of the cross.

Back in the bedroom, Aaron shaves, a towel wrapped around his waist. He tells me he wants to go to the village nearby. I'm up for anything. My eyes snag on the heater again, its hulking bulk, like a creature waiting to pounce. I must have been wrong about the hunting scene. Sure, there's the white stag and the maiden in red, but birch trees and pines surround them, pretty yellow flowers and songbirds at their feet.

A bird trills from our window. Aaron's been talking all this time as he layers fleece on top of fleece, ties the laces of his hiking boots. Outside, the ground is wet from last night's rain, although the sky glistens blue. At the gates, I turn to look back at Castle B—. The tower windows are opaque with sunlight and shadows cross the courtyard. A glimpse of red on the parapet—so bright for a moment then gone quickly. *Did you see that?* I ask, but Aaron points to a building mirroring the shape of the castle in miniature. *The mirror maze. We'll go there later.* The double wooden door to the maze resembles a closed mouth.

We wind down the hill, cross a bridge over a fast-moving river to the village, and climb narrow twisted streets to the main plaza. A covered wooden staircase leads from the main plaza up a hill to the Ivory Church (*One-hundred and ninety-nine stairs,* Aaron informs me, as if he's a walking guidebook), and older women in headscarves—indistinguishable from the crone and the cook—grip shopping bags and trudge across the cobblestones, girls in high heels and short skirts sit at café tables in the sun and drink small twisted bottles of the local brand of Coke.

We visit the supermarket to buy bottled water and boxes of dry chocolate cookies. There, the shelves are sparsely stocked, the goods pushed forward to the edges of the shelves to hide the bareness behind. *This is what it must've looked like under communism*, I say.

There was a dictator here, he says. *Fascism, not communism.* This country has been free only two years, the length of our marriage. During our honeymoon (days spent in bed, nights at the resort's bar), the news was occupied with the demonstrations in the country. The iconic video on all the news channels after protestors stormed the President's Palace: the dictator and his wife running to their private jet, suitcases full of plunder, her fluttery red scarf blowing behind her, as they escaped to Russia.

When Aaron climbs the covered staircase to the Ivory Church, I sit at a café, the table rocking on uneven pavement, and take out my notebook from my purse. Hoping a change in scenery will spark some poetry. I order coffee, although caffeine so late in the day may keep me awake all night.

There's a pattern in the cobblestones on the plaza, circles among circles: a labyrinth. I wonder how old it is, the story behind it, and write in my notebook, *labyrinth*. My table jostles as a man sits down, although other tables are empty. He wears a jean jacket over a T-shirt with the Mercedes logo and reeks of alcohol, alcohol soaked into his skin, exuding out of his pores, as if he's bathed in beer and vodka and the bitter herbal liquor this country is known for. Not handsome but in a way that's hot, like the famous actor who was born here. He must have been on quite a bender, and I nod at him approvingly. When he lights a cigarette, I'm worried it may ignite him too.

You stay at the castle? he says. *You are the winner?*

I nod. *You speak English?*

I worked once in London. Deported. He adds something that sounds like a curse word, and then, *but here I am back again.*

He flags down a waiter and orders *pivo*. He asks me if I am American, how much a plumber makes there (I make up a number), and what I do (when I say poet, he says, *We all need more beautiful words*). The waiter brings him a tall gleaming amber beer.

He's older than I originally thought, wrinkles feathering from the corner of his eyes and lips. But still hot, if I look a little away from him, notice how his long fingers circle his glass, the way he throws back his head when he laughs at something he says, his squint as he gazes at me.

I'd be lying if I tell you it's been a while since I flirted with a man not my husband.

Have you seen the Red Lady yet? he says.

Tell me about her.

He shrugs. *The usual stories. She committed suicide, was enclosed into the castle walls, or got lost in the maze. A woman left by her man, a woman pregnant with a bastard, a woman who murdered her husband, a woman murdered by her husband. What does it matter?*

It very much matters, who did the leaving, who did the murdering. But I say, *Have you seen her?*

No, what would a drunk like me be doing up at the castle?

Suddenly hostile, he chugs the rest of the beer and slams the mug down on the table.

I'm sorry, I say. His reaction must be my fault. He stalks away, without paying for his beer, cigarette pinched between thumb and index finger, bumping first into the table and then into my husband as he leaves.

Already picking up men? Aaron says. He sits down, spreads his legs under the small table so I need to adjust mine. Panting a little after the one-hundred and ninety-nine steps. *You've lowered your standards.*

I twist the wedding ring on my finger. *You know me, making friends wherever I go.*

Yes, he says. *I know you.*

Geez, Aaron, he didn't even speak English.

I'm sorry, he says. *I didn't mean to say that. But can you blame me?*

I take that as a rhetorical question. Yes, I could blame him. No, I am full of guilt.

He calls for the check and throws a stack of bills on the table. I close my notebook. There's the one word I'd written, *labyrinth*, and a maze around it, like the mazes I drew in high school when I was bored, curving tight lines and pathways resembling the wrinkles and folds on a brain. I hadn't even realized I was drawing.

The sun sets as we hike up to Castle B—. When we pass through the castle gates, I say, trying to broach the distance between us, *Let's go to the mirror maze.*

It'll be better in the daylight.

Aaron, I ask, *do you know the story of the Red Lady?* We were in the kitchen then, eating venison stew and dumplings, and I mop the gravy, rich with blood, with a chunk of brown bread.

You didn't even read the website for Castle B—, did you?

Just tell me. Don't make me read it on my phone.

He sighs. *Vladislav of B— took a wife, Margosha, and sired a son by her. Vlad thereafter died in battle, and, left alone, she "went crazy," as the website says. She hired young boys and girls from the village as servants and killed them. She used their blood to dye her clothes and to feed the stags in Castle B—'s parks. The villagers revolted, and, ultimately, her teenage son slayed her.*

That drunk from the café said her husband may have murdered her.

I thought he didn't speak English. Silence settles heavy between us. I'm not going to apologize—except to myself, for not remembering my lie. *Why do I even bother, Lucy?* He throws his cloth napkin on the table, storms out of the kitchen.

I push the remainder of the stew around my plate, then put the dishes in the sink, as the Manual instructs. I am exhausted, barely able to walk up the stairs and crawl into the big canopy bed. Aaron sits propped up with pillows and watches Netflix with his AirPods on, ignoring me. Thunder echoes across the valley.

When I dream, I dream that Aaron sleeps next to me, his laptop nestled between us, and the green curtains of the bed are drawn around the bed, enclosing us in a jade box. I slip out and the porcelain stove exudes waves of heat, although I didn't light it before going to bed. The tiles pulse the dark red of dried blood. A low moan from the hallway and I open the door (I know this is a dream because I would huddle under the covers if I were awake) and a red skirt flashes down the stairway. I follow it, a woman, in a red dress, a veil slithering down her spine, walking—no *floating*—through corridors that are white-washed and ones that are not, through a dining room with mounted stags' heads and a huge stuffed bear, through an armory with walls covered with swords, up and down stairways, but no matter how fast I run, I cannot catch up to her. Up another spiral staircase, and I'm in a solarium, one wall of windows and a view of the dark valley below, and the Red Lady is nowhere to be seen.

I realize I'm awake, in my pajamas. My hands press against the cold glass of the window. Across the valley, under the moonlight, the walls of the church gleam. I have no idea how to find my way back though the dark castle to the bedroom suite. I huddle on a silk-upholstered settee, half falling into sleep, watching the moonlight ignite the small dust motes in the air. I think of hands that aren't Aaron's caressing me. When the sky lightens from pale purple to orange to vivid red and then to blue, I walk through what I believe is the entirety of the castle, and I find our empty bedroom suite and dress.

The stove is cold to the touch. The images on the tile are still, but now there's no hunting scene, no forest scene, but a maze snaking around the sides and front, men and women lost within. For what seems like a long while, my eyes follow the paths of the maze, seeking to solve it, but I cannot. I tear myself away from the stove. I don't know what's going on, and I don't want to know; I want to fast-forward to this afternoon, when the driver takes us to the university city, where I've reserved the honeymoon suite, in an excess of optimism, at the fanciest hotel.

Aaron's in the kitchen, reading his phone, his empty plate pushed away from him. The cook bustles around him, clucks at me, and cracks two eggs into a cast iron pan.

Where were you?

I got up early to wander around. Sorry to worry you.

Oh, I wasn't worried, you always land on your feet. He continues to scroll through his phone, laughing under his breath. I refuse to ask him what he thinks is so funny. After the cook slides the eggs on my plate, he sets the phone down. *We have just enough time to go to the labyrinth.* He takes my hand, squeezes it. I take this as another gesture of forgiveness, but I'm not sure if I am willing to accept. *I want us to solve it together.*

I imagine us holding hands as we exit the mirror maze. He waits for me to finish breakfast and then leads me to the mirror maze and opens its dark carved wooden doors with a brass barrel key, the bow of the key fashioned into a stag's head. *This was built in 1830. The lord sought to trap his younger brother in the maze. He was sent in and never came out. After, children mostly used it, until the Red Lady was seen.*

I step inside. Carved wooden pillars frame mirrors and arch to a ceiling also covered in mirrors. The light is slippery, golden. There are so many of me in the mirrors. So many of him. Reflections hover in silvery glass, in the tarnished corners: in one reflection, we hold hands, in another, we flinch apart, in another, I am with a man I recognize, in yet another, I am with a man I don't. The reflections are infinite. My fingers trail on the surface of the mirrors, seeking solidity and empty space. We find an opening, follow a path. In the corner of my eye, a flutter of red scatters across the surfaces of the mirrors.

Aaron's reflection skitters across the face of a mirror and then disappears. I am alone. One of the mirrors in my path is cracked and my fingers snag on the sharp edge. A thin line of blood wells up. Hysteria rises in my chest. I move quicker, bump into a sheet of clear glass between two columns. I turn to find the path, my hands outstretched.

The mirror in front of me reflects a woman, her veil thrown back, her eyes like coals, her garments not merely red but flames. Her veil and dress flowing lava. Whether divine flame or the flames of hell, she is the most awesome creature I have ever seen, her light so bright I cannot look directly at her. I fall to my knees. The maze strobes red. *Are you cursed or are you blessed?* she says. Her voice echoes. *Cursed,* I think. *Guilty as charged.* And then she disappears, or, rather, is extinguished, and only an afterimage of light lingers then fades. The gleaming mirrors still surround me. I call for Aaron. But there's only my image, multiplied sixfold.

[contributor bios]

Lori Sambol Brody lives in the mountains of Southern California. Her short fiction has been published in *Smokelong Quarterly*, *Wigleaf*, *Tin House Flash Fridays*, the *New Orleans Review*, *Craft*, *The Rumpus*, and elsewhere. Her stories have been chosen for the *Best Small Fictions* 2018 and 2019 and *Best Microfiction* 2021 anthologies. She can be found on Twitter at @LoriSambolBrody and her website is lorisambolbrody.wordpress.com.

Samuel Clark is a 2019 alum of the University of North Carolina Wilmington, where he graduated with an MFA in fiction. He is the recipient of the LGBTQ+ writer scholarship for The Muse & The Marketplace 2019, a partial scholarship recipient to Sundress Academy for the Arts, and a 2021 candidate for the *Kenyon Review* Writers Workshop. He lives in Colorado with his adopted cat, Emily D.

Ted Hayden's stories have appeared in literary publications including *Newfound Journal* and genre publications including *Nature: Futures*. Read more of his work at tedhaydenstories.com

[contributor bios]

Aimee Herman is the author of the novel, *Everything Grows* (Three Rooms Press) and two full length books of poems, *meant to wake up feeling* (great weather for MEDIA) and *to go without blinking* (BlazeVOX books), in addition to being widely published in journals and anthologies including *BOMB*, *Cream City Review*, and *Troubling the Line: Trans and Genderqueer Poetry and Poetics* (Nightboat Books). Aimee is a queer writer and educator and a founding member in the poetry band, Hydrogen Junkbox.

Erica Kent lives in Portland, Maine with her family and chunky bulldog. She's a devoted but irreverent high school English teacher and tutor. Her work has appeared in *StoryQuarterly*, *The Brooklyn Rail*, and *The Maine Review*, among others.

Kaleena Madruga received her BA in Creative Writing from San Francisco State University and her MFA in Creative Writing from Roosevelt University. She lives in Chicago.

Lyndsie Manusos's fiction has appeared in *SmokeLong Quarterly*, *The Magazine of Fantasy & Science Fiction*, *Passages North*, and other publications. She lives in Indianapolis with her family and writes for Book Riot and *Publishers Weekly*.

[contributor bios]

Cassidy McFadzean is an incoming fiction candidate at Brooklyn College. Her stories have been published in Hobart, carte blanche, PRISM international, and The Best Canadian Stories 2020.